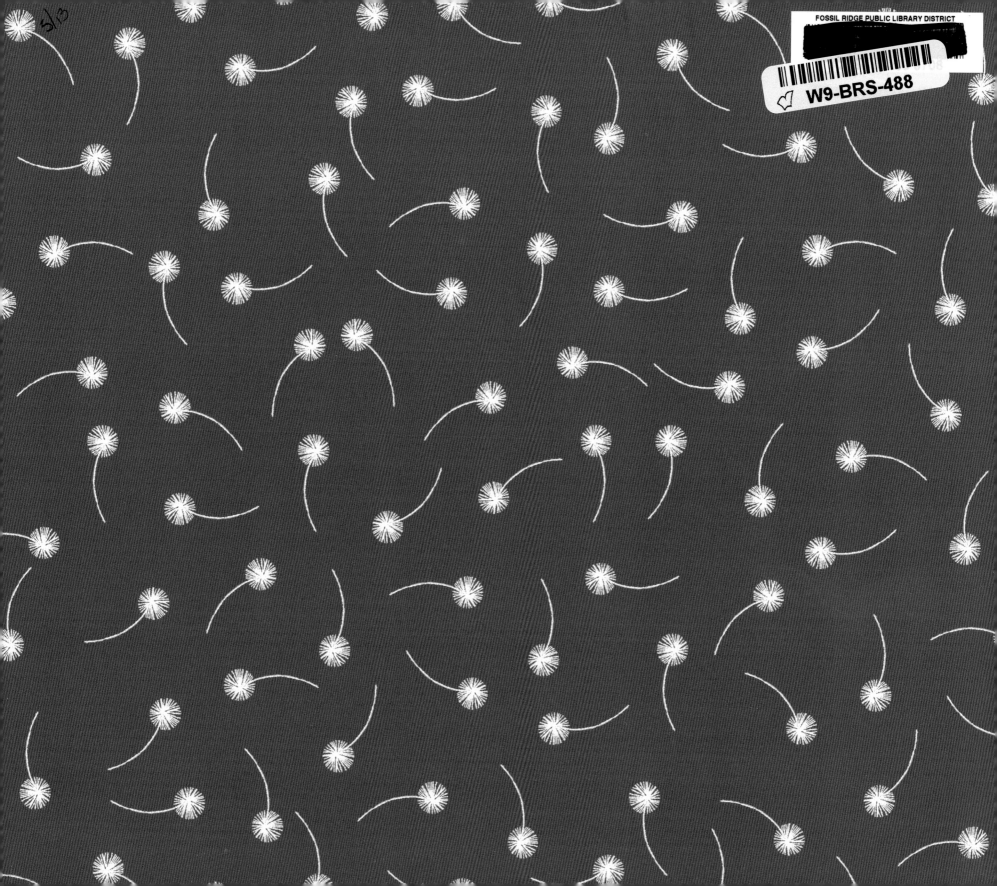

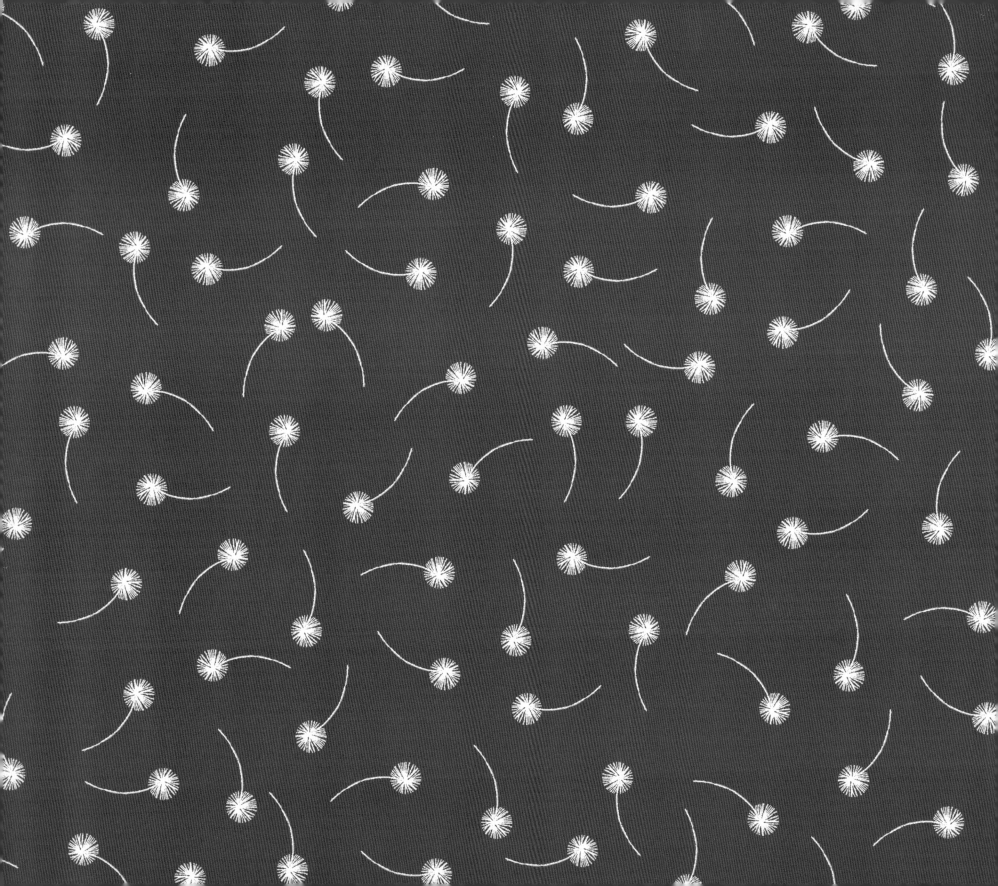

I dreamt...

A book about hope

First published in Spanish as *Soñé que las pistolas disparaban mariposas* by Artes de México
Text copyright © 2012 by Gabriela Olmos
Copyright © 2012 by Artes de México
First published in English in Canada and the USA in 2013 by Groundwood Books
English translation copyright © 2013 by Elisa Amado

Groundwood Books / House of Anansi Press
110 Spadina Avenue, Suite 801, Toronto, Ontario M5V 2K4
or c/o Publishers Group West
1700 Fourth Street, Berkeley, CA 94710

We acknowledge for their financial support of our publishing program the Canada Book Fund (CBF).

Library and Archives Canada Cataloguing in Publication

Olmos, Gabriela
        I dreamt— : a book about hope / written by Gabriela Olmos ; illustrated by Manuel Monroy ... [et al.] ;
translated by Elisa Amado.

Book created by Mexican artists as a fundraiser for the IBBY Fund for
        Children in Crisis.
Translation of: Soñé que las pistolas disparaban mariposas.
ISBN 978-1-55498-330-8

        1. Children and violence—Juvenile fiction. I. Monroy, Manuel
II. Amado, Elisa III. Title.

PZ7.O53I 2013   j863'.7   C2012-905752-5

Design by Alejandra Guerrero Esperón
Printed and bound in China

I dreamt...
A book about hope

Gabriela Olmos

Translated by Elisa Amado

Groundwood Books

I dreamt of **Pistols** THAT SHOOT *butterflies...*

and that SOLDIERS prefer shadowboxing

14

to **shooting** at each other.

15

And in my dream **bombs** were

BURSTING OUT

in

gales of *laughter*.

and that **danger** could be cut into *confetti* if only you could find the RIGHT PAIR of SCISSORS.

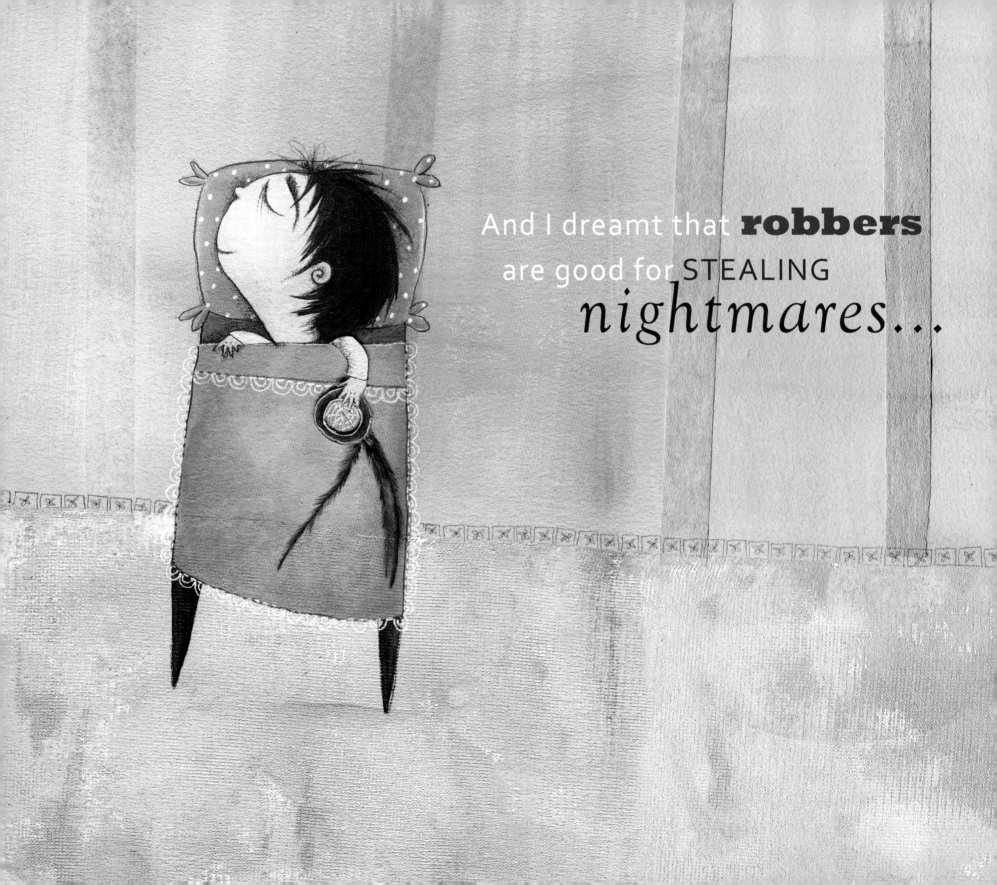

And I dreamt that **robbers** are good for STEALING *nightmares…*

while *jokes* are the best way to DRIVE a **kidnapper** away.

24

When I WOKE UP I remembered that for many KIDS life is more of a **nightmare** than a sweet *dream.*

And that it will always be that way
UNLESS we *kids*

choose TO LEARN from city *trees...*

SOME of whom are crushed by the pavement.

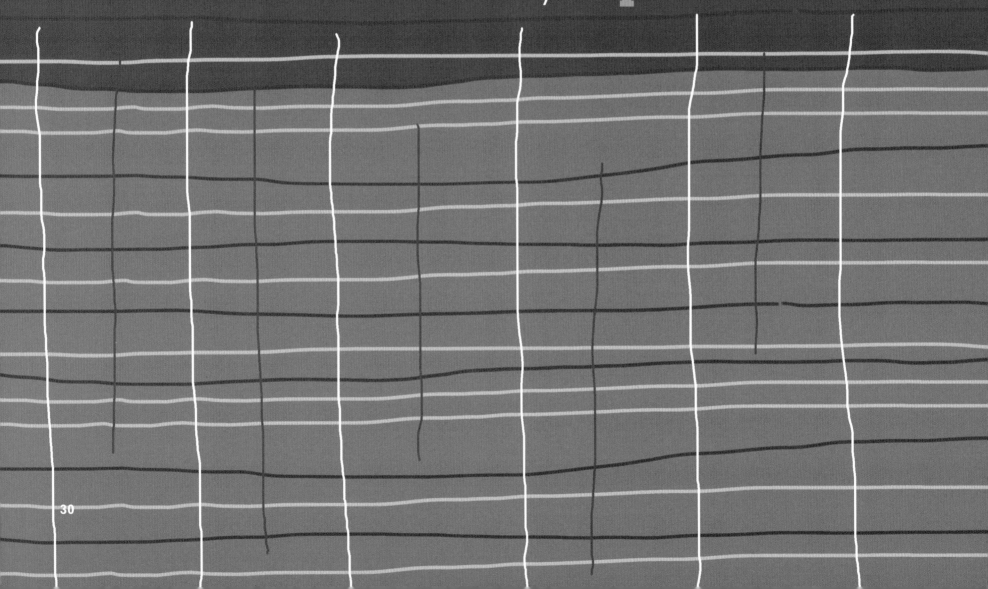

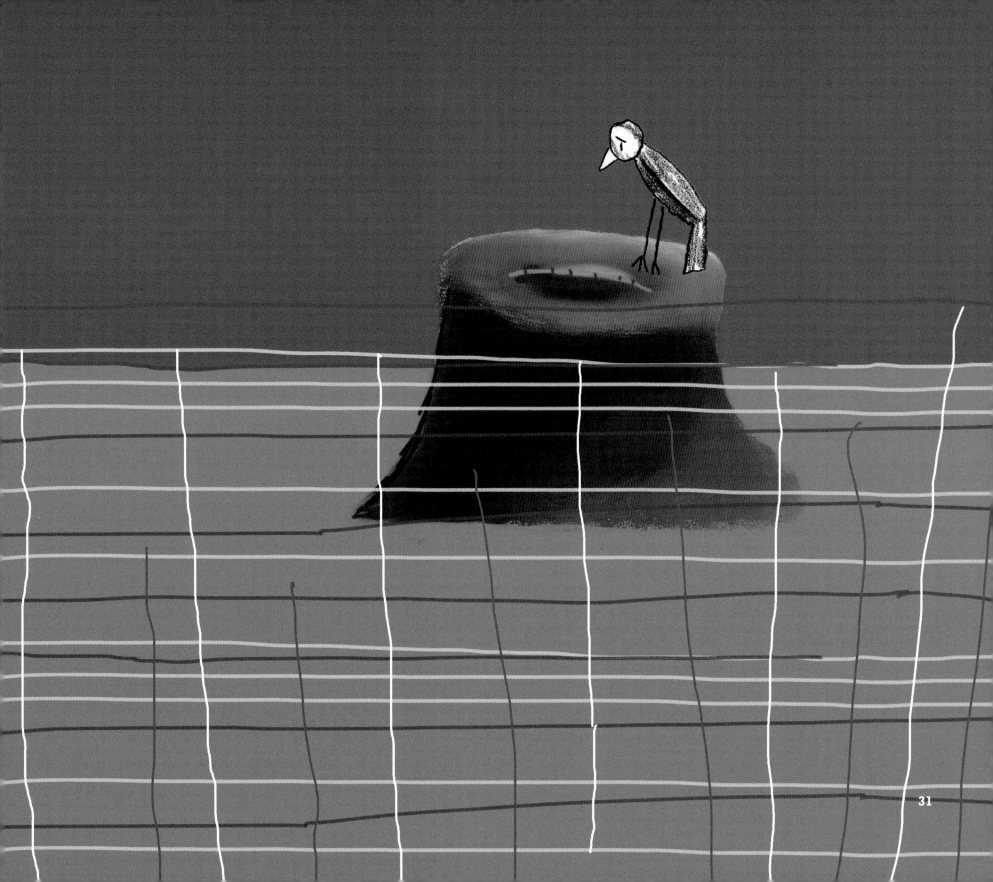

But I know others who *fight back* and BREAK OPEN the **sidewalks...**

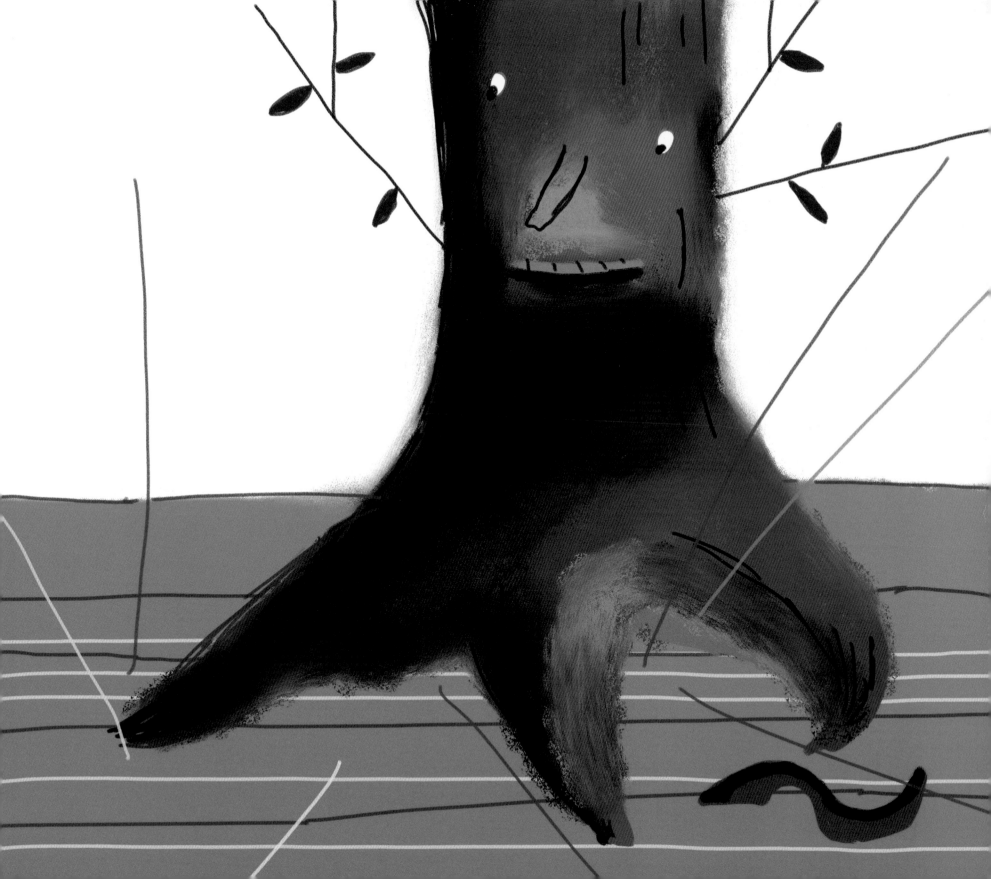

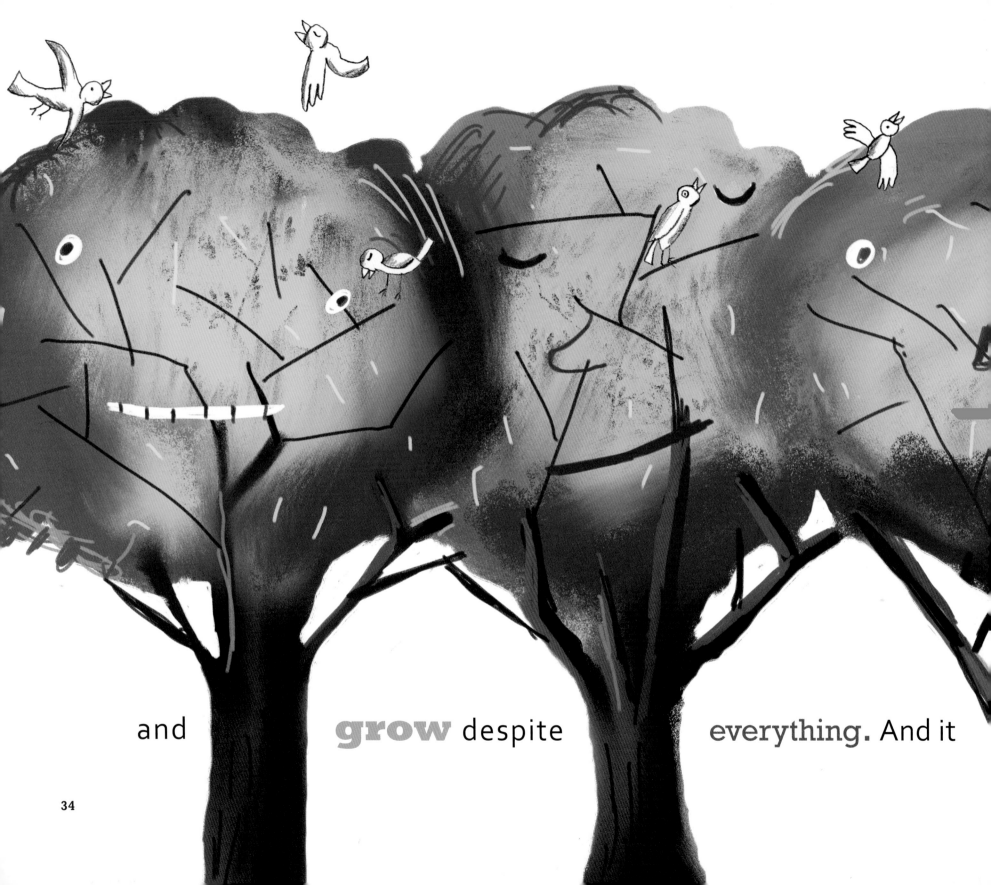

and **grow** despite everything. And it

is they who help us   all to *breathe*.

I dreamt...

A book about hope

In many parts of the world, including North America, children live with violence. Wars, gangs, guns, crime, bullying, harassment and fear keep many kids from living the full, free lives that every child should enjoy.

This book was created in Mexico, where for the past six years a vicious war against drugs has brought fear and insecurity into every child's life. Many children's dreams have become nightmares. Some of Mexico's best illustrators have donated their art to create this book, which gives children a way to talk about their fears, a reason to hope, and the inspiration to resist falling into grief and depression. Like some city trees they have the possibility to grow strong and, despite everything, to try and make the world a better place.

I dreamt... is being published in North America for the same reasons. Royalties from sales will be donated to the International Board on Books for Young People—IBBY's Fund for Children in Crisis—which supports bibliotherapy projects that use books and reading to help children who have lived through wars, civil conflicts and natural disasters to think and talk about their experiences.